GW00870520

For Ellie and Charlie. Xx

And little Woody. xx

Once upon a time, there was a handsome, happy boy called Charlie. His favourite food in the world was toast. He could eat it all day long.

He was on the way to see his friend Daisy when he decided to take a shortcut through the park.

It wasn't long before Charlie got lost. He looked around, but all he could see were trees. Nervously, he looked into his bag for his favourite toy, Snowy.

Snowy was a fluffy snow leopard. Charlie had had him since he was a toddler.

But Snowy was nowhere to be found! Charlie began to panic. He felt sure he had packed Snowy. To make matters worse, he was starting to feel hungry.

Unexpectedly, he saw three hairy dogs disappearing into the trees.

"How odd!" thought Charlie.

For the want of anything better to do, he decided to follow the shifty-looking dogs.

Perhaps it could tell him the way out of the forest.

Eventually, Charlie reached a clearing. He found himself surrounded by houses made from different kinds of food. There was a house made from bread, a house made from crisps, a house made from biscuits and a house made from doughnuts Charlie could feel his tummy rumbling. Looking at the houses did nothing to ease his hunger.

"Hello!" he called. "Is anybody there?"
Nobody replied.
Charlie looked at the roof on the closest house and wondered if it would be rude to eat somebody else's chimney. Obviously, it would be impolite to eat a whole house, but perhaps it would be considered acceptable to nibble the odd fixture or lick the odd fitting, in a time of need.

A cackle broke through the air, giving Charlie a fright. A witch jumped into the space in front of the houses. She was carrying a strange bubble. In that bubble was Snowy!

"Snowy!" shouted Charlie. He turned to the witch. "That's my toy!"
The witch just shrugged.
"Give him back!" cried Charlie.
"Not on your nelly!" said the witch.
"At least let him out of that bubble!"

Before she could reply, three Hairy dogs rushed in from a footpath on the other side of the clearing. There was a big dog, a medium-sized dog and a small dog.

Charlie recognised the three dogs from earlier. The witch seemed to recognise him too.

"Hello Big Dog," said the witch.

"Good morning." The dog noticed Snowy. "Who is this?"

"That's Snowy," explained the witch.

"Ooh! He would look lovely in my house. Give it to me!" demanded the dog.

The witch shook her head. "He is staying with me.

"Um... Excuse me..." Charlie interrupted. "Snowy lives with me! And not in a bubble!"

Big Dog ignored him. "Is there nothing you'll trade?" he asked the witch.

The witch thought for a moment, then said, "I do like to be entertained. I'll release him to anybody who can eat a whole front door."

Big Dog looked at the house made from doughnuts and said, "No problem, I could eat an entire house made from doughnuts if I wanted to."
"That's nothing," said the next dog. "I could eat two houses."
"There's no need to show off," said the witch. Just eat the front door and I'll let you have Snowy.
Charlie watched, feeling very worried. He didn't want the witch to give Snowy to Big Dog. He didn't think he would like living with a Naughty dog, away from his house and all the other toys.

The other two dogs watched while Big Dog put on his bib and withdrew a knife and fork from his pocket.

"I'll eat this whole house," said Big Dog. "Just you watch!"

Big Dog pulled off a corner of the front door of the house made from crisps. He gulped it down smiling and went back for more.

And more.

And more.

Eventually, Big Dog started to get bigger – just a little bit bigger at first. But after a few more fork-fulls of crisps, he grew to the size of a large snowball – and he was every bit as round. "Erm... I don't feel too good," said Big Dog. Suddenly, he started to roll. He'd grown so round that he could no longer balance!

"Help!" he cried, as he rolled off down a slope into the forest.

Big Dog never finished eating the front door made from crisps and Snowy remained trapped in the witch's bubble.

The medium-sized dog stepped up and approached the house made from biscuits.

"I'll eat this whole house," She said. "Just you watch!"

The second dog pulled off a corner of the front door of the house made from biscuits. She gulped it down smiling and went back for more.

And more.

And more.

After a while, she started to look a little queasy.
She grew greener...
...and greener.

A woodcutter walked into the clearing. "What's this bush doing here?" he asked.

"I'm not a bush, I'm a dog!" said the dog, who was now feeling very ill.

"It talks!" exclaimed the woodcutter. "Those talking bushes are the worst kind. I'd better take it away before somebody gets hurt."

"No! Wait!" she cried, as the woodcutter picked her up. But the woodcutter ignored her cries and carried the dog away under his arm.

The medium dog never finished eating the front door made from biscuits and Snowy remained trapped in the witch's bubble.

Little Dog stepped up and approached the house made from doughnuts.

"I'll eat this whole house," said Little Dog. "Just you watch!"

Little Dog pulled off a corner of the front door of the house made from doughnuts. He gulped it down smiling and went back for more.

And more.

And more.

After five or six platefuls, Little Dog started to fidget uncomfortably on the spot.

He stopped eating doughnuts for a moment, then grabbed another forkful. But before he could eat it, there came an almighty roar. A bottom burp louder than a rocket taking off propelled Little Dog into the sky.

"Aggghhhhhh!" cried Little Dog. "I'm scared of heigh..."

Little Dog was never seen again. Snowy remained trapped in the bubble.

"That's it," said the witch. "I win. I get to keep Snowy."

"Not so fast," said Charlie. "There is still one front door to go. The front door of the house that's made from Bread. And I haven't had a turn yet.

"I don't have to give you a turn!" laughed the witch. "My game. My rules."

The woodcutter's voice carried through the forest. "I think you should give him a chance. It's only fair."

"Fine," said the witch. "But you saw what happened to the dogs. He won't last long."

"I'll be right back," said Charlie.

"What?" said the witch. I thought you wanted your silly toy back."

Charlie ignored the witch and gathered a hefty pile of sticks. He came back to the clearing and started a small campfire. Carefully, he broke off a piece of the door of the house made from Bread and toasted it over the fire.

Once it had cooked and cooled just a little, he took a bite. He quickly devoured the whole piece. Charlie sat down on a nearby log.

"You fail!" cackled the witch. "You were supposed to eat the whole door."

"I haven't finished," explained Charlie. "I am just waiting for my food to go down."

When Charlie's food had digested, he broke off another piece of the door made from Bread. Once more, he toasted his food over the fire and waited for it to cool just a little. He ate it at a leisurely pace then waited for it to digest.

Eventually, after several sittings, Charlie was down to the final piece of the door made from Bread. Carefully, he toasted it and allowed it to cool just a little. He finished his final course. Charlie had eaten the entire front door of the house made from Bread.

The witch shouted angrily. "You must have tricked me!" she said. "I don't reward cheating!"

"I don't think so!" said a voice. It was the woodcutter. He walked back into the clearing, carrying his axe. "This little boy won fair and square. Now hand over Snowy or I will chop your broomstick in half."

The witch looked horrified. She grabbed her broomstick and placed it behind her. Then, huffing, she popped the bubble.

Charlie hurried over and grabbed his lovely toy, checking that his favourite toy was all right. Fortunately, Snowy was unharmed.

Charlie thanked the woodcutter, grabbed a quick souvenir, and hurried on to meet Daisy. It was starting to get dark. When Charlie got to Daisy's house, his friend threw her arms around him. "I was so worried!" cried Daisy. "You are very late.

As Charlie described his day, he could tell that Daisy didn't believe him. So he grabbed his bag and pulled out a huge napkin.

"What's that?" asked Daisy.

Charlie unwrapped a doorknob made from crisps and more doughnuts that they could eat. "Pudding!" he said. Daisy almost fell off her chair laughing.

The End............Or is it?

This book could not have been made without the support of my beautiful wife and children.

Thank You.
X X X

Printed in Great Britain
by Amazon

64512671R00020